DOG █████

"There's Mrs. Briar!" Joe said. He pointed to the neighbor who lived across from them. She was standing the middle of her front yard. Joe thought she looked lost. "Hi, Mrs. Briar!" he shouted. "Is anything wrong?"

Mrs. Briar turned at the sound of Joe's voice. "Yes, there is, boys," she called to them. "Charlie has disappeared!"

THE HARDY BOYS®

SECRET FILES #7

The Disappearing Dog

BY FRANKLIN W. DIXON

ILLUSTRATED BY SCOTT BURROUGHS

ALADDIN ▪ NEW YORK LONDON TORONTO SYDNEY

This book is a work of fiction. Any references to historical events, real people, or real locales are used fictitiously. Other names, characters, places, and incidents are the product of the author's imagination, and any resemblance to actual events or locales or persons, living or dead, is entirely coincidental.

ALADDIN

An imprint of Simon & Schuster Children's Publishing Division

1230 Avenue of the Americas, New York, NY 10020

First Aladdin paperback edition October 2011

Text copyright © 2011 by Simon & Schuster, Inc.

Illustrations copyright © 2011 by Scott Burroughs

All rights reserved, including the right of reproduction in whole or in part in any form.

ALADDIN is a trademark of Simon & Schuster, Inc., and related logo is a registered trademark of Simon & Schuster, Inc.

THE HARDY BOYS is a registered trademark of Simon & Schuster, Inc.

For information about special discounts for bulk purchases, please contact Simon & Schuster Special Sales at 1-866-506-1949 or business@simonandschuster.com.

The Simon & Schuster Speakers Bureau can bring authors to your live event.

For more information or to book an event contact the Simon & Schuster Speakers Bureau at 1-866-248-3049 or visit our website at www.simonspeakers.com.

Designed by Lisa Vega

The text of this book was set in Garamond.

Manufactured in the United States of America 0516 OFF

10 9 8 7 6 5

Library of Congress Control Number 2011930733

ISBN 978-1-4424-2314-5

ISBN 978-1-4424-2315-2 (eBook)

✦✦ CONTENTS ✦✦

1

Class Magician

Nine-year-old Frank Hardy's substitute teacher for the week, Ms. Yung, came into the room, a big smile on her face, and said, "I've just come from the principal's office, students. You're getting a new classmate! He used to go to the school where I taught last year, so I already know all about him."

Frank leaned over to his friend Callie Shaw and whispered, "Whoever it is must be really something."

Just then a boy appeared at the classroom door.

He was dressed in a knit shirt, jeans, and sneakers. He was holding a green backpack in his left hand. Frank wondered what was so special about this average-looking kid.

"This is Max O'Malley, class," Ms. Yung announced. "And he has a very special talent."

Max smiled at the class.

"Our principal said I could let Max show you what it is," Ms. Yung continued. "Would you like that?"

"Yeah," a few kids said sleepily.

Ms. Yung nodded at Max, and he ran out of the room. Frank gave Callie a puzzled look. Before he could say anything, though, Max was back. But now he had a black top hat on his head, a black cape around his shoulders, and a long black wand in his left hand.

"Class," Ms. Yung announced, "I give you Max O'Malley, Magician!"

When nothing happened, Max said, "This is where I usually get loud applause!"

Frank looked at Callie and rolled his eyes.

"Knock, knock! Hello!" Max said. "I'm waiting!"

Several kids at the front began to applaud weakly. Then the applause increased to the point that it was at least polite.

"Thanks!" Max said. With a swirl of his cape he swept into the room and stood to the side of Ms. Yung's desk. "I can make *anything* disappear!" he said. *"Anything!"* He slowly narrowed his eyes to slits. "So you all need to be careful!"

"Oh, brother," someone in the class mumbled.

Suddenly Max took off his top hat and waved his wand over it, and a puff of smoke whooshed from inside.

"You're not supposed to light anything on fire on school grounds!" Emily Franklin shouted.

Ms. Yung stood up. "Emily, there is no fire here," she said. "It's part of Max's magic act." She looked around the room. "Wasn't that just fantastic, class? Let's give Max a big hand!"

This time the class clapped louder than before. And Frank had to admit that he hadn't expected smoke to come out of Max's hat. But he wanted to see some more tricks before he was really impressed with the class's new member.

Ms. Yung said, "Now we'll have an intermission and take the geography quiz I scheduled for today." She turned to Max. "You don't have to take it now if you don't want to, since you didn't know about it."

"Oh, that's no problem, Ms. Yung. I love geography," Max said. He hung his cape and hat on a coat hook. "In fact, in between my shows I relax by reading geography."

Callie leaned over and said to Frank, "I can't decide if I like this kid or not."

"I know. He's making it hard. I want to like him," Frank replied.

The geography quiz was mostly about China, Ms. Yung's parents' home country before they moved to the United States. Frank thought he knew all the answers.

After the quiz Ms. Yung made another announcement. "Well, class, I thought I'd let Max treat you to the rest of his magic show before we go out for recess. Would you like that?"

Everyone applauded enthusiastically!

Max headed to the front of the room. He took his cape off the hook and put it around his shoulders. When he set the top hat on his head, though, there was a sound: *Cheep! Cheep! Cheep!* A silly grin appeared on Max's face. He took the top hat off, stuck his hand inside it, and pulled out a baby chick. "Well, what do you know?" he said. He showed the chick to the class.

There were several oohs and aahs, and then everyone applauded again.

For the next several minutes Max walked around the room, pulling a quarter out from behind Ms. Yung's ear, a dime out from behind Callie's ear, and a penny out from behind Frank's ear.

"My ear is worth more than a penny!" Frank complained.

Max shrugged. "What can I say?" he told the class. "I don't decide how valuable your ears are. I just pull out whatever coin I find there."

Frank looked over at Callie. "For some reason I don't think Max likes me," he whispered.

Just then the recess bell rang. Everyone started filing out of the classroom.

"Why don't you put on a magic show for some of the other kids?" Frank asked Max as they started out the door. "I know my brother, Joe, and his friends would really enjoy it!"

"Sure! Why not?" Max said. "I'm always looking for new fans!"

Max followed Frank and Callie outside.

Frank spotted Joe and some of his classmates dribbling basketballs on the outside court.

"Joe! Put away the basketballs!" Frank shouted

to his brother. "We have a surprise for you."

Joe and his friends turned and looked at Max dressed in his magician's outfit.

Max stood under one of the baskets. Joe and his basketball buddies formed a row in front of him. They were soon joined by kids from some of the other classes.

"I'll introduce you, Max," Frank whispered. He turned to the audience. "Ladies and gentlemen, I give you the one, the only, Max O'Malley, Magician!" He and Callie began applauding, and they were joined by the rest of the audience.

Then Frank turned to Max and nodded. "The stage is all yours!" he said.

Max went through his usual routine and was an immediate hit. Frank was a little miffed that Max pulled a quarter from Joe's ear. He was sure Max did it on purpose.

Finally, just as Max was bringing his show to

a close, someone called out, "Can you make *people* disappear?"

Max got a funny look on his face, grinned, then suddenly turned toward Frank. "I can make *anyone* disappear."

2

How Did Charlie Disappear?

n the way home from school all Joe wanted to talk about was Max O'Malley.

"He's really cool, Frank," Joe kept saying.

"He's all right, I guess," Frank said.

Joe stopped and looked at his brother. "Okay. Spill it," he said. "Are you just jealous, or is there more to the story?"

Frank explained the feeling he had about Max. "It's really strange," he concluded. "I've never met him before, but he makes me feel as if he knows all about me and that he doesn't like any of it."

"It's show business, Frank!" Joe said.

Frank shrugged. "Yeah, I guess," he admitted.

"Do you know what I'm thinking about?" Joe said as they continued walking toward home.

"What?" Frank asked.

"Who I would like to see Max make disappear," Joe said with a grin.

Frank grinned back. "Adam Ackerman!"

Adam Ackerman was the biggest bully in Bayport, and he was always making trouble for Frank and Joe.

Frank let out a sigh. "That's too much to hope for," he said, "but if Max really can make people disappear, Adam Ackerman is the first person I'd volunteer!"

Just then Frank and Joe turned onto their street.

"There's Mrs. Briar!" Joe said. He pointed to the neighbor who lived across from them. She was standing the middle of her front yard. Joe thought she looked lost. "Hi, Mrs. Briar!" he shouted. "Is anything wrong?"

Mrs. Briar turned at the sound of Joe's voice. "Yes, there is, boys," she called to them. "Charlie has disappeared!"

Charlie was Mrs. Briar's prizewinning Chihuahua. "Did you say he's *disappeared*?" Frank asked her when they got closer.

Mrs. Briar nodded. "I can't imagine where he went," she said. "I put him out in the backyard, as I do every afternoon in good weather, so he can get his exercise. But when I went to call him for supper, he wasn't there anymore."

Frank looked at Joe. "You don't think it's possible that . . . ," he began.

Joe finished with, "Max made Charlie disappear?" He thought for a minute. "Why would he do that for no reason at all?"

Frank shrugged. "It's just a feeling," he said. He turned back to Mrs. Briar. "Well, your backyard is awfully big, Mrs. Briar. Why don't you let Joe and me take another look for you?"

"Oh, that is so kind of you boys," Mrs. Briar said. She gave them a big smile. "I know the Hardy

boys are famous in Bayport for solving all kinds of mysteries, and this is certainly a mystery." She let out a big sigh. "I just hope Charlie isn't unhappy about anything," she added. "There's an important dog show coming up in a couple of weeks." She looked at Frank and Joe. "You don't think he's run away, do you? Because he doesn't want to compete?"

Frank shook his head. "I don't think so, Mrs. Briar," he said. "Joe and I have seen Charlie at some of the shows."

"Yeah!" Joe said. "He's a real competitor!"

With Mrs. Briar in the lead, the Hardy boys headed for her backyard.

Mrs. Briar's love for her backyard was third only to her love for Charlie and dog shows. The yard was huge. Frank and Joe remembered how they used to play there when they were younger and would often get lost themselves. It was surrounded by shrubs, and rosebushes that always seemed to have huge blossoms. There was a sunken patio that the Briars used to use for entertaining the neighbors. Thick shrubbery lined the tall wooden fence all the way around the yard.

"I don't see how Charlie could have gotten out of this yard, Mrs. Briar," Frank finally said. "I've seen pictures of prisons that would be easier to escape from!"

"Oh my goodness, Frank," Mrs. Briar said. "Do you think Charlie considers my backyard a prison?" She turned and surveyed the grounds. "I always thought it was more like a beautiful park."

"Frank didn't mean he thought your backyard was a prison," Joe said hurriedly. "He just meant we can't see any way that Charlie could have escaped."

"But he did, Joe," Mrs. Briar said sadly. "He just *disappeared.*"

There's that word again: "disappeared"! Joe conveyed his thought to Frank with just a look.

"It's a mystery, all right, Mrs. Briar," Frank said.

"And you can be sure that Frank and I will try to solve it," Joe offered.

"Oh, boys, thank you so much," Mrs. Briar said.

"We'll start by looking around the neighborhood," Frank said.

3

Magic Secrets

Frank and Joe crossed the street and went inside their house.

They found their mother in the kitchen, a book in one hand, a mixing spoon in the other. Mrs. Hardy was a librarian. No matter what else she was doing, she was always holding a book.

"Hello, boys," Mrs. Hardy said. She looked at the clock over the stove. "I was beginning to wonder why you weren't home yet."

"We were across the street talking to Mrs.

Briar," Joe said. "Charlie has disappeared."

"*Disappeared?*" Mrs. Hardy said. "How in the world did he get out of that backyard?"

"That's what we were wondering too, Mom," Frank said.

"But we helped Mrs. Briar search every inch of it," Joe added, "and Charlie was nowhere to be found."

"That's terrible," Mrs. Hardy said. "Mrs. Briar lives for the dog shows, and Charlie always wins."

"We told her we'd help her solve the mystery," Frank said. "Do we have time to do some sleuthing before Dad gets home for dinner?"

"You're in luck. Your father just called and said he'd be late. He's meeting with some Bayport police detectives about a case," Mrs. Hardy said. Although Mr. Hardy was a private investigator with his own cases, he often used his expertise to help the local police solve theirs. "It'll probably be at least another hour before he gets home."

"That should be enough time for us to question the neighbors," Frank said. He turned to Joe. "Right?"

"That sounds like a plan," Joe said.

Chet and Iola Morton now lived one block over from the Hardys. They had moved in from the country the year before. Frank knew that Mrs. Morton loved dogs. She would have noticed one wandering around in her front yard.

Iola answered the door. "Hey, Frank! Hey, Joe! I can't do your homework now, but if you'll come back . . ."

"Funny, Iola," Frank said. "Really funny!"

"I'm glad you thought so," Iola said. "I had just started mapping out my comedy tour when the doorbell rang."

"Cool, Iola," Joe said. "Do you need a manager?"

Iola grinned. "What are you guys up to?" she asked. "Chet's not here, if he's the one you wanted to talk to. He's helping Dad."

"We're looking for Charlie, Mrs. Briar's dog,"

Frank said. "He's disappeared. We thought maybe your mom might have seen him wandering around your yard earlier."

"Charlie! That dog's worth a lot of money," Iola said. "Are you sure he wasn't stolen?"

"Well, Charlie is gone, so 'disappeared' could mean stolen," Joe said, "or it could mean something else, which we're not ready to discuss yet."

"You two can be so secretive at times," Iola complained.

"That's the life of a detective for you, Iola," Frank said. "What can I say?"

"Whatever!" Iola said. "Mom!" she shouted.

Mrs. Morton hurried into the room. "What's the matter, Iola? . . . Oh, hi, boys! Chet isn't—"

"They're looking for Charlie, not Chet, Mom," Iola said. "He's disappeared."

"Oh, that's terrible!" Mrs. Morton said. "His family must really be upset!"

"Charlie is a dog, Mom," Iola said.

"Oh," Mrs. Morton replied. "Well, it's still terrible."

"Did you see or hear a Chihuahua in your yard earlier today, Mrs. Morton?" Joe asked.

Mrs. Morton shook her head. "No, I'm sure there was no Chihuahua around," she said. "They're not exactly quiet dogs, so I would have noticed."

Frank looked at his watch. "We should be going," he said. "We promised Mrs. Briar we'd ask all around the neighborhood for her."

"Thanks, Mrs. Morton," Joe said. He turned to Iola. "Just let me know when your tour bus is leaving, and I'll be here," he added.

Iola grinned. "You got it," she said.

Mrs. Morton gave them both puzzled looks.

During the next thirty minutes they stopped at the houses of some of their other neighborhood friends to ask about Charlie.

Belinda Conrad's mother said she'd been shopping most of the day.

Biff Hooper's father had stayed home from the office because of a terrible migraine and had slept most of the day.

Tony Prito said both of his parents were still at work, so no one would have been around to see a wandering Chihuahua.

"Well, what do we do now?" Joe said as they stood in front of Tony's house trying to determine their next move. "Except for Adam Ackerman, we've asked all the people we know around here, so . . ."

"I wonder who lives there now," Frank said.

"Lives *where*?" Joe asked.

"See that brick house down the street, the one where the shrubs need to be trimmed badly?" Frank said. "The For Sale sign is gone."

"I hadn't noticed," Joe said. "It was empty a long time."

"Let's find out," Frank said. "We've got a good excuse ⸻ ⸻ doorbell."

The ⸻ ⸻ headed down the street.

"Wow!" Joe said. "This front yard looks like a jungle!"

"We could get lost in here and never find our way back," Frank added.

Together, they pushed their way through the overgrown shrubbery, mounted the front steps, and rang the doorbell.

When the door finally opened, they were both speechless for a minute.

Finally Joe said, "Max the Magician!"

Max grinned. "In the flesh," he said. "If you're looking for another magic show, though, you'll have to pay for it!"

Frank bit his tongue to keep from saying what he was thinking. "No, we're looking for a missing dog," he said. "It's a prizewinning Chihuahua named Charlie."

"It belongs to our neighbor, Mrs. Briar," Joe added. "Have you seen it? Or have your parents?"

Max just grinned at them for a moment, then said, "Why? Did it *disappear*?"

Frank and Joe looked at each other.

"Yes, Max," Frank said. "That's why we're asking you!"

Max continued to smile. "Sorry," he finally said as he started to shut the door, "but I don't discuss my magic secrets with anyone!"

4

What's the *Why*?

Frank and Joe stood on Max's front porch staring at the closed door.

"If you made Charlie disappear, Max," Joe shouted, "that's a crime!"

"Joe!" Frank said. "Who are you talking to?"

"I bet he's still standing there behind the door," Joe told his brother. "He's probably waiting to see what we're going to do next."

"We're going to go home, that's what," Frank

said. "We need to talk to Dad about what our next move should be."

"Good idea," Joe said.

Mr. Hardy was pulling into the driveway when Frank and Joe got to their house.

"Hello, boys!" Mr. Hardy shouted to them as he got out of his car. "Are you just now getting home from school?"

"No, sir," Joe said. "We've been looking for Charlie."

"You mean Charlie has disappeared?" Mr. Hardy asked.

Frank nodded. "That's exactly what we mean, Dad," he said, "and we need to talk to you about the exact meaning of the word 'disappeared.'"

Mr. Hardy blinked. "Well, I must say, this sounds like a perfect conversation for the dinner table," he said, "so let's go inside and get ready."

• • • •

After Mr. Hardy changed clothes, he joined the rest of the family in the dining room.

"It's Italian night," Mrs. Hardy informed them. She held up a book. "I've been reading this wonderful novel set in southern Italy. The different kinds of pizzas the family ate sounded so delicious that I got a book on Italian cooking, and . . . well, here they are."

"They look and smell wonderful, dear," Mr. Hardy said. He took a slice of the first pizza and passed the pan to Frank and Joe.

"That's Pizza Margherita, named for Queen Margherita of Italy in 1889," Mrs. Hardy said. "It has tomato sauce, mozzarella cheese, and basil." She smiled. "Red, white, and green: the colors of the Italian flag!"

Mrs. Hardy pointed to a second pan. "And that's a Roman pizza," she said. "It has a thin crust and not as much cheese."

For the next several minutes, while Mrs. Hardy gave everyone the history of pizza, Frank, Joe, and Mr. Hardy helped themselves to slices of other types from around Italy.

After they had all finished eating, Mrs. Hardy held up another book and said, "I'm starting this novel tomorrow. It's set in Moscow. So next week be prepared for a Russian dinner!"

"We'll be ready, Mom!" Frank and Joe said.

"That goes for me as well, dear," Mr. Hardy said. He turned to Frank and Joe. "Okay, let's talk about the disappearance of Charlie. From what you told me outside, you think 'disappearance' has another meaning in this particular case."

Frank and Joe nodded.

Frank told their parents about his new classmate, Max O'Malley, and how Max was practically a professional magician.

"Well, he sounds like a really interesting young man," Mrs. Hardy said.

"I think he's a jerk," Frank said.

Mr. Hardy looked at him. "Frank! That's not a very kind thing to say."

"Sorry, Dad," Frank said. "I guess we should explain."

"That's always a good idea," Mrs. Hardy told them.

"At school Max said he could make *anyone* disappear," Joe said, "but I guess we all thought he was just bragging."

"We even joked about his making Adam Ackerman disappear," Frank added.

Mr. Hardy raised an eyebrow but didn't say anything.

"When we got home, Mrs. Briar was standing on her front lawn. She told us that Charlie had disappeared," Joe continued. "After we searched her backyard, we went around the neighborhood asking if anyone had seen him."

"No one had, until we got to that house a couple of blocks away," Frank explained. "You know the one, with the shrubs in front that make it look like a jungle . . ."

"Oh goodness, yes!" Mrs. Hardy said. "It's terrible!"

"Well, we knocked on the front door, and Max answered," Joe said. "When we told him that Charlie had disappeared, he just grinned, making us think he was the one who had done it. And when we asked him if he had, all he said was that he never discussed his magic secrets with anyone."

"Max sure did make a lot of things appear and

disappear at school, Dad," Frank said, "so we think he could be behind what happened to Charlie."

Mr. Hardy rubbed his chin, then said, "Let's start with the six *W*s."

Frank and Joe nodded. Several years ago their father had told them that the starting point for all cases, including the ones he worked on, should be with the answers to What, When, Where, Why, Who, and How—the six *W*s. At first Joe had protested that "How" didn't begin with *W* like the other words, but then Frank pointed out that it ended with *w*, which was just as good.

"What is the disappearance of Charlie," Joe said.

"When is this afternoon," Frank added.

"Where is Mrs. Briar's backyard," Joe said, "and Why . . ."

Just then the telephone rang, and Frank excused himself from the table to answer the extension in the kitchen. When he came back, he said, "That was Mrs. Briar. She said Charlie is home. He suddenly *reappeared* in her backyard."

"Well, well, well; that's really strange," Joe said. "It must have happened right after we talked to Max."

Frank thought for a minute. "I guess the Who is Max, and the How is magic . . ." He paused. "What we need to figure out now, though, is the Why!"

5

Snack Solution

The next morning at school Frank spotted Max near one of the slides.

"How did you find him so fast?" Joe asked Frank.

"I looked for a crowd," Frank said with a grin. "I knew Max would be in the center of it."

"Come on," Joe said. "Let's see what he's up to now."

As they approached, Max noticed them and grinned.

"Smart move making Charlie reappear, O'Malley," Frank said.

"But most people in Bayport don't like it when their pets disappear," Joe added.

Now Max gave them an even bigger grin.

"Did you make someone's pet disappear, Max?" one of the second graders asked. "That is so cool."

"No, it's not!" Frank told him. "How would you like it if one of your pets disappeared?"

The second grader turned to him. "I can't stand my sister's cat. It's mean! It's always scratching me." He turned back to Max. "Do you think you could make it disappear?"

"We'll talk later," Max told him.

"Max!" Joe yelled, but Frank pulled him away.

"This isn't going to do any good," Frank whispered. "He's playing to the crowd now, Joe. He'll say anything."

"Yeah, I know," Joe finally agreed.

"Come on," Frank said. "We'll just keep an eye on him during the day. That's all we can do for now."

"You're right," Joe said. He shook his head. "I'm sure he's going to try something else."

In class Frank made sure he watched Max's every move. For the most part Max stayed in his seat, but since everyone was working on independent projects that included interviewing other members of the class, it was hard to keep up with everything Max was doing. He was almost always surrounded by other classmates.

"He did it," Frank muttered. "I know he did."

"Well, well," Callie said, "Frank Hardy can actually talk."

Frank turned to her. "What did you say?"

"I've been asking you the same question for at least the last ten minutes, Frank," Callie said, "and you haven't made a sound until this minute." She frowned. "Are you all right?"

"No, I'm not all right," Frank whispered to her.

"Spill it," Callie whispered back.

Frank told her about Max and Mrs. Briar's dog. "Joe and I are sure he made Charlie disappear, and then reappear when he thought we were going to report him."

"Really?" Callie asked.

Frank nodded. "Of course, he never actually admitted it," he added. "He just kept giving us one of those silly grins." He frowned at Callie. "Did you say you needed to ask me a question?"

Callie nodded. "I'm doing my project on the need for more bicycle paths in Bayport," she said. "What do you think?"

"I'm in favor of them," Frank said. "Joe and I like to ride our bikes after school. But the traffic in our part of town can be scary."

Callie took notes. "Okay," she said. "Now, how do you feel about Bayport's requiring everyone to give up automobiles for a day and only ride bicycles?"

Frank thought for a minute. "Oh, I don't know, Callie," he said finally. "I don't like thinking of my mom and dad on bicycles. It's not a pretty sight."

Callie giggled. "I think I'll forget that question," she said.

• • • •

For the rest of the day, while they were in class, Frank made sure he knew everything Max was doing. Once they were outside, Joe took over. It was obvious they were the only two who were suspicious of Max. Everyone else seemed to think he was the coolest student in school.

Max had an endless supply of tricks. When he wasn't pulling eggs and quarters out of people's ears, he was pulling baby chicks and rabbits out of his top hat.

Even the teachers thought Max was terrific.

"I think it's a losing battle, Frank," Joe whispered when he met his brother in front of the school for the walk home. "Max can do no wrong if you listen to what everyone else is saying."

"Detectives don't give up, Joe," Frank said. "That means *we're* not giving up!"

"Hey, look!" Joe whispered. "There's Max now!"

Frank looked down the street. Max was saying

good-bye to some of the other kids, who were acting as though his leaving were the end of the world.

"I think I'm going to throw up," Joe said.

"There's no time for that now, Joe," Frank said. "We need to follow Max to make sure he doesn't make someone else's pet disappear!"

Frank and Joe gave Max enough of a head start that he'd only know he was being followed if he turned around and stared back down the street. From time to time, though, they hid behind bushes if they thought Max was getting suspicious.

"Do you think he knows we're following him?" Joe whispered.

"It's hard to tell with him," Frank whispered back. "We just need to be careful."

Frank and Joe weren't prepared for Max's twirls, though. All of a sudden Max whirled around, facing in their direction, but instead of calling out to them he gave a couple of quick bows.

Frank and Joe dived for the nearest shrub.

"Aw, man!" Frank whispered. "He must have known we were following him all along."

"I don't think so, Frank," Joe whispered back. He peered through the branches of the shrub. "He's still giving bows."

Frank frowned. "Let me see," he said, looking. "I can't believe it," he marveled. "He's practicing for his magic show. Wow! Is he full of himself or what?"

They sat behind the shrub for a few more minutes, then peeked out again to see if Max had started back down the street.

"Where did he go?" Joe said.

"You've got to be kidding me," Frank said. "He just disappeared!"

"I'm beginning to hate that word," Joe said. "Come on. Let's go home."

Just as the Hardys turned onto their street, though, they saw Mrs. Briar out in her front yard again.

"Oh no," Frank said. "I don't like the looks of this!"

"Mrs. Briar!" Frank called. "Is everything all right?"

"No, it isn't!" Mrs. Briar called back. "I put Charlie outside to get some fresh air, but when I went to give him his favorite snack, he wasn't there anymore!"

"Max!" Joe muttered.

"His favorite snack!" Frank exclaimed. "That's how we can get Charlie back, Joe!"

6

The Horrible Smell

I think we figured out how to get Charlie back," Frank said to Mrs. Briar. "We need some of his favorite snacks."

"Well, I guess I could do that," Mrs. Briar said, "but how will you know where he is to give it to him?"

"Is this the snack that he always goes crazy for?" Joe asked. He remembered being in Mrs. Briar's backyard once when Charlie almost knocked him down to get this treat.

"Well, this is a new one, Joe, not the one you might remember," Mrs. Briar said with an embarrassed grin. "It's made from liver, mostly. I think it has a horrible smell, but Charlie thinks it's the most wonderful thing on earth!" She pointed to the porch. "There's the box. Take as many as you want if you think they'll bring my precious Charlie back home!"

"Oh, I'm sure this will work," Frank said. He winked at Joe. "We have a plan all figured out."

Before they were halfway to the porch, Joe said, "Whoa—is that smell coming from the treats?"

Mrs. Briar smiled. "Yup," she said. "They're kind of strong, aren't they?"

"Yes, ma'am!" Frank managed to gasp.

Frank and Joe looked at each other. They weren't sure now that this plan would work, but there was no turning back. They had told Mrs. Briar they would return Charlie. So they'd just have to put up with one of the worst odors they had ever smelled.

Mrs. Briar poured a cupful for Frank and one for Joe. "Now, boys, I don't usually give Charlie this many at once, although I'm sure he'd eat them," she said, "but it might take almost this many to coax him back from wherever he keeps going."

"Thanks, Mrs. Briar," Frank said. He was trying not to gag.

Joe swallowed hard and managed to add, "We'll get him back for you, Mrs. Briar!" *Even if it kills us,* he thought, *and right now I'm almost sure it will!*

Frank and Joe hurriedly left Mrs. Briar's backyard.

"Oh, man, have you ever smelled anything so awful?" Joe said. "What's with that dog, that he likes this stuff?"

"There's no accounting for taste," Frank said. He stopped and looked around. "Fill all your pockets with these snacks, and then we're going to—"

"Are you nuts?" Joe exclaimed.

"Joe! This plan is foolproof. I know what I'm doing," Frank said decidedly. "We'll not only get Charlie back, we'll expose Max for the fake he is!"

"Hey!" Joe said. "I can live with that!" He took a deep breath and held it while he stuffed his pockets with the liver treats. Frank did the same.

"Now then, we're going to Max's house," Frank said, "and when we get there, just follow my lead."

"Okay, brother, I'm in your hands," Joe said.

Frank and Joe walked as fast as they could down the street, around a corner, and down two more blocks until they reached Max's house. Joe rang the bell.

When Max answered, Frank pushed past him, saying, "We came to apologize. We want to be friends, Max! Why don't you show us your room?"

Stunned, Max just stood at the front door as Joe rushed in too.

"We need to get the scent of these snacks all over the house," Frank whispered to Joe, "so that Charlie will smell it and start barking."

"Gotcha," Joe whispered back.

"What are you two doing?" Max demanded. He had shut the front door and was standing with his hands on his hips. "What's going on?"

"We're trying to be your friend, Max," Frank said.

"I bet your room's upstairs," Joe said. "Come on, we want to see it!"

Frank and Joe hurried up the stairs.

Max was right behind them. "What's that awful smell?" he demanded.

"What smell?" Frank said.

"I don't smell a smell!" Joe added.

"It's awful!" Max said. "It's the worst smell I've ever smelled."

"I bet this is it," Frank shouted. He was standing

at an open door. Inside, the room looked like back-stage at a magic show. There were black capes and black top hats on wall hooks, and cages with chicks and rabbits. "Come on, Joe! Let's look around!"

Joe followed Frank inside Max's room. He made a big circle. No Charlie.

"You two are weird!" Max said.

"What about your backyard?" Frank asked. "We'd like to see your backyard."

"Yeah!" Joe chimed in. "Maybe sometime we could play football over here after school."

Downstairs, the front door slammed shut.

"Max! Max! What is that horrible smell?" a woman's voice shouted. "Where are you?"

Max arched his left eyebrow. "I'm upstairs with a couple of *friends*, Mother," he shouted.

Frank and Joe looked at each other as Mrs. O'Malley seemed to take the stairs two at a time. When she reached the three of them, she stopped and sniffed. She looked at Frank and Joe, got closer, and then sniffed again.

"Young men, I do not mind if you come to our house to play with Max," Mrs. O'Malley said, "but you must take baths first!" She backed away. "I'm sorry, but you smell terrible!"

Frank felt himself blushing. He nodded to Joe, and together, they went downstairs. Max followed.

Once outside on the O'Malley's front porch, they could hear Max laughing and laughing and laughing.

"This will be all over school tomorrow, won't it, Frank?" Joe said.

"Yep!" Frank said. "Some detectives we are!"

7

Chased!

Just as Frank and Joe stepped off the O'Malley's front porch to head back home, they heard, "Bruno! Stop! Stop!"

Frank looked down the street and saw a huge brown dog pulling an elderly man holding a leash. They were both headed straight for the boys.

"I think that poor man needs our help, Joe," Frank said.

Right before the man and the dog got to them, though, the man yelled, "Do you boys have some of those new liver treats in your pockets? They're the only things that make Bruno go crazy like this!"

"Yes, we do!" Frank shouted. "Do you want Bruno to have them?"

"No! No! Bruno loves them, but they make him sick!" the man shouted. "Run! Run! Please don't let him get them from you!"

Frank and Joe took off running, but the man and Bruno were right behind them.

Up ahead Joe saw a young girl who had a large black dog on a leash. All of a sudden the dog started barking frantically and began pulling the young girl toward Frank and Joe.

"What else is in these dumb treats besides liver?" Joe said. "I've never seen dogs go insane before!"

"Me neither," Frank agreed, "but we'd better change direction fast."

They ran across the street, cut through a front yard, and jumped a low fence that bordered an alley. But they could still hear the frantic wailing of the dogs rushing to get the liver treats. The dogs were getting closer and closer.

"I don't think we can make it home before they attack us!" Frank said. He looked around, trying to get his bearings. "Hey! Chet and Iola live on the other side of this street. Come on!"

Frank and Joe ran down the alley. Just as they reached the next street, they saw the two dogs, dragging their owners behind them, at the other end of the alley.

"I hope the Mortons are home," Joe said as he and Frank raced for the front porch. He rang the doorbell. The dogs had reached the street and were both heading straight for the porch. Their owners were nowhere in sight. "Chet!" Joe shouted.

Just then Chet opened the front door and let Frank and Joe inside. When he saw the dogs, he said, "What did you two do to them?"

"Shut the door!" Frank yelled. Now the dogs were on the porch, barking furiously and pawing at the screen door. "We didn't do anything!"

Chet looked around. "What's that horrible smell?" he asked. He looked at Frank and Joe and sniffed. "Hey! It's coming from you two! What's going on here?"

Just then the dogs' owners arrived, grabbed the leashes, and began pulling the dogs away from the house.

"I guess they can't smell the treats anymore," Joe said.

"Wow!" Frank said. He looked at Chet. "It's a long, long story, friend, and we'll tell you about it, but first we need one of those garbage bags that absorbs odors!"

No one else was at home at the Mortons', so Chet took care of disposing of the liver treats and sprayed the house with room freshener to get rid of the odor. Frank and Joe showered while Chet put their clothes in the dryer with several sheets of scented fabric softener.

When Frank and Joe were dressed, they came downstairs, where Chet was waiting for them at the kitchen table with sodas.

"I smell like roses," Joe complained.

"Yeah, I know," Chet told him. "Isn't it great? It's so much better than liver!"

Frank laughed.

Joe wrinkled his nose.

"Okay, tell me what's going on!" Chet said. "When you two are involved, it's always interesting."

"Charlie has disappeared," Frank began, "so we were trying to get him back." He told Chet about Max's reaction when they'd first told him that Charlie was missing. "We were just sure that Max was using a magic trick to do it."

"Well, where do the dog treats fit in?" Chet asked.

"Mrs. Briar said Charlie craves them," Joe explained. "We thought if we filled our pockets with treats and went to Max's house, Charlie would go crazy trying to get them, and we'd solve the mystery of his disappearance."

"Instead, we managed to stink up the O'Malleys' house," Frank continued, "and Mrs. O'Malley said we could only play with Max if we went home and took baths."

"It was really embarrassing," Joe said.

"Well, I see Charlie isn't the only dog who goes nuts over those treats," Chet said.

Frank nodded. "That's how we ended up here," he said.

"If Max really did take Charlie, hoping people would think he *magically* made him disappear," Joe said, "then I'm sure now, after what just happened, he's going to make it impossible for us to find him until he's ready to make Charlie *magically* reappear."

"Maybe Max really can make animals disappear," Chet said.

"Max isn't really that good, I don't think," Frank said. "In fact, I'm beginning to wonder if maybe someone else is actually behind this, and if maybe Charlie has just been smart enough to escape on his own from wherever he's being held prisoner." He shook his head. "The problem is, how many more times will Charlie be able to do that? We have to find the dognapper before it's too late."

"We both thought Max was a jerk," Joe said. "So that made it easy for us to think he was behind Charlie's disappearance."

Frank nodded. "But our evidence is only circumstantial," he said. "We don't have *real* evidence."

Frank and Joe stood up.

"We need to go home and make a list of new suspects," Joe said.

Frank grinned at Chet. "Thanks for saving our lives!"

Chet grinned back. "That's what friends are for."

8

Suspect Number One— Again!

Frank and Joe headed to Mrs. Briar's house. "We need to find out who in the neighborhood doesn't like Charlie," Frank said. "Then we'll have some other suspects to question."

Joe rang Mrs. Briar's doorbell. Immediately he heard barking inside.

"Oh, hi, boys," Mrs. Briar said when she opened the door. "Charlie is back home."

"That's wonderful," Frank said. He wanted to add, *But for how long?* But he didn't. "May we visit with you for a minute? It's about Charlie."

"Of course, boys," Mrs. Briar said. She opened the screen door. "Come on inside, and I'll give you each a glass of lemonade."

"That sounds wonderful," Joe said. He loved Mrs. Briar's lemonade.

Frank and Joe followed Mrs. Briar to her sunporch.

"Have a seat, boys," she said, "and I'll be right back."

Mrs. Briar soon returned with a pitcher of her secret-recipe lemonade and poured three tall, frosty glasses.

Charlie lay at her feet.

Everyone took a long sip of the lemonade, and then Mrs. Briar said, "Now then, boys, what's on your minds?"

"We believe that someone is taking Charlie from your backyard," Frank began, "and then somehow Charlie manages to escape, but . . ."

"We're not sure how much longer your dog will be able to do that," Joe continued, "so we're wondering if you know of anyone who doesn't like Charlie."

"Goodness, boys, I can't imagine anyone not liking Charlie enough to do something like *kidnap* him," Mrs. Briar said. She shook her head. "I'm afraid I won't be able to help."

"Charlie is a wonderful dog, Mrs. Briar," Frank said, "but some people, well, they just don't—"

"Wait a minute!" she said. "My neighbor's grandson . . . oh, no, he wouldn't kidnap Charlie just for that."

"Let us do the investigating, Mrs. Briar," Joe said. "That's our job."

"And you boys do have a wonderful reputation in Bayport," she said. "All right. Well, Mr. Buster and his grandson, Johnny Buster, live across the alley from me. Johnny shows dogs too. But he's never won. Charlie always places ahead of any dog Johnny's showing."

Joe wrote down Johnny Buster's name in his notebook. They now had a new Who. "Anyone else, Mrs. Briar?" he asked.

"Now that you have me thinking about this, there is a young man named Phillip Stanley, whom I hired to walk Charlie once a day," Mrs. Briar said, "but he quit after a week when I wouldn't pay him more."

"I've heard of him," Frank said.

Joe wrote Phillip's name under Johnny's. Then he stood up and looked over at Frank. "We'd better talk to both of these suspects as soon as possible," he said.

Mrs. Briar walked Frank and Joe to the front door. "I hope you find out who's doing this, boys," she said.

"We'll do our best," Frank told her, "and thanks for the lemonade."

Frank and Joe hurried around to the other side of the block and rang Mr. Buster's bell. After several minutes a teenage boy opened the door and said, "What are you selling?" He had a cast on his leg and was leaning on a crutch.

"We're not selling anything," Frank told him. "We're just helping Mrs. Briar, the lady who lives across the alley from you. Her dog, Charlie, keeps disappearing, and we're wondering if you've noticed anyone suspicious in the neighborhood this week."

"No, I haven't, but ever since my accident I can't walk around much," Johnny said. He gave Frank and Joe a long, hard look. "Is she blaming me?"

"Oh, no," Joe said hurriedly. "We just told her we'd check around the neighborhood, that's all."

"Well, I never have liked that dog because he's always beating my dogs," Johnny said, "but I certainly wouldn't want any harm to come to him."

"Well, thank you," Frank said. "We're sorry to have disturbed you."

Back on the sidewalk Joe said, "There's no way he could have taken Charlie, so that leaves Phillip Stanley." Joe rubbed his chin just the way their father did when he was thinking. "How do you know this guy, Frank?"

"I don't. But his younger brother goes to our school," Frank said. "I overheard him in the hall the other day telling someone Phillip works in that new supermarket a couple streets over."

"Off we go!" Joe said.

When Frank and Joe got to Riverview Market, they found Phillip cleaning up the eggs from a carton someone had dropped.

"Aren't you Jordan Stanley's older brother?" Frank asked him.

"That's right," Phillip said. "What can I do for you guys?"

"Uh, well, we live across the street from Mrs. Briar," Joe said, "and we used to see you walking her dog, Charlie."

"We haven't seen you doing it lately," Frank continued, "so we were going to ask her if we could have the job to earn some extra money. But we wanted to know why you quit."

"Is she hard to work for?" Joe asked.

"Oh, no, she's one of the nicest ladies you'll ever meet," Phillip said.

"That's always been our impression too," Frank said.

"But I'm trying to save money for college, and Mrs. Briar couldn't pay me more," Phillip continued, "so when I turned sixteen last week, I quit and took this job."

"That makes sense," Joe said.

Outside, Frank and Joe stood for a minute.

"Are you thinking what I'm thinking?" Frank asked.

"If you're thinking we talked ourselves out of believing Max was a suspect just because we were embarrassed at his house," Joe replied, "then yes, I am!"

"Real detectives don't do that, Joe," Frank said.

"And that means we shouldn't either," Joe added. "Max O'Malley is back to being Suspect Number One!"

9

The Big Magic Show

And I know exactly how we're going to catch him, too," Frank said. "We're going to put on a big magic show in Mrs. Briar's backyard!"

"What?" Joe said.

"Think about it, Joe!" Frank said. "Mrs. Briar loves doing things for the neighborhood kids, so why wouldn't she want to have a magic show for them?"

"Keep going, Frank," Joe said. "This is beginning to get interesting."

"Since Max will be the star," Frank said, "he won't be able to resist returning to the scene of the crime."

"Ah, yes, I get it now," Joe said. He nodded and gave Frank a big grin. "Criminals often return to the scene of a crime to relive it—or to see if they left any evidence behind."

"And sometimes they can't keep from confessing, because they want to show you how smart they are," Frank added.

"That describes Max, all right," Joe said. "He thinks he's smarter than everyone else. But what if he doesn't confess? What if he just has a good time and goes home?"

"I've got that worked out too, Joe," Frank said. "Then it'll be up to Charlie."

Joe got a puzzled look on his face. "What do you mean by that?" he asked.

"When Max gets to Mrs. Briar's house, Charlie will either run up and start barking angrily at him, if Max was mean to him," Frank said, "or—"

"Or," Joe interrupted excitedly, "Charlie will rush up to him, panting excitedly, expecting a treat, if Max bribed him when he made Charlie 'disappear'!"

"Exactly!" Frank said. "We have all bases covered!"

"Let's go talk this over with Mrs. Briar," Frank said. "We need to have the magic show as soon as possible!"

They hurried over to Mrs. Briar's house.

"Well, boys, have you solved the mystery already, or are you back for some more lemonade?" Mrs. Briar asked when she opened the door. "There's still a half pitcher left."

"Neither, ma'am," Frank said. "We want to talk to you about having a party."

"A party? What fun!" Mrs. Briar said. "Come on in!"

They told Mrs. Briar all about their idea, and she loved it. "Let's have hamburgers and hot dogs and . . . oh, goodness!" Mrs. Briar stood up. "I'm going to need some help!"

After the boys left Mrs. Briar's, Joe said, "I just thought of something. What if Max doesn't want to do the show? What if he says no?"

"Then we'll have him for sure," Frank said. "Max loves the spotlight, so if he turns down this gig, there can only be one reason."

Joe nodded. *"He doesn't want to return to the scene of the crime!"*

"Exactly!" Frank said.

• • • •

The next day at school Frank stopped Max in the hall on the way to their class. He handed Max a flyer that he and Joe had made the night before, advertising the magic show at Mrs. Briar's.

"I know we should have asked you first," Frank said, "but when we told Mrs. Briar how great you are, she immediately started planning a magic show!"

Max looked at the flyer, then looked at Frank, then looked back at the flyer. "Is this for real?" he asked. "It's not another one of your silly detective stunts?"

Frank bit his tongue to keep from getting angry. "Sorry about the smell at your house," he said. "No, this is for real. Just talk to any of the kids in our neighborhood and they'll tell you how great Mrs. Briar's parties are!"

Max handed the flyer back to Frank. "I'll do that," he said.

Frank watched Max continue on down the hall toward their classroom. *Is our plan going to work,* he wondered, *or will Max outsmart us this time too?*

All morning Frank kept his eye on Max. Max talked to several students in the class, but Frank didn't know if he was talking to them about the party or the projects they were working on.

Finally, when the recess bell rang, Max came over to Frank's desk and said, "I'll do it! I think it'll be a lot of fun!"

Frank exhaled. "You bet it will!" he said. "We'll enjoy every minute of it!"

For the next few days, after school Frank and Joe made the invitations and delivered them around the neighborhood. On Friday afternoon before the Saturday morning party, they helped set up a small canvas tent and a stage in front of it.

When they were finished, Frank and Joe admired their work.

"It's a great setting for solving a mystery, isn't it, Frank?" Joe said.

"Perfect," Frank agreed.

Saturday morning Frank and Joe hurried over to Mrs. Briar's house to help her with last-minute preparations. They found her in the backyard. She was sitting at her patio table just staring into space.

"What's wrong, Mrs. Briar?" Joe asked when they reached her.

"Charlie has disappeared again," Mrs. Briar said.

10

Secret File #7:
Magically Solved

e's playing us for suckers, Frank!" Joe exclaimed angrily.

"That's for sure," Frank agreed. "Well, we'll show him who the *real* sucker is!"

"Boys!" Mrs. Briar exclaimed. "What's the matter?"

Joe looked down at Mrs. Briar and said, "Uh, nothing. It's just that—"

"Hey, everybody! I'm here!"

Frank and Joe looked up. Iola Morton was coming through the gate. Chet was right behind her.

"We'll get Charlie back for you, Mrs. Briar," Frank whispered to her. "You can be sure of that!"

"Thank you, boys," Mrs. Briar said. She stood up slowly. "I'd better put on my hostess face. I want everyone to have a good time." She motioned to Iola. "Over here, dear! Come tell me all you've been up to lately!"

During the next several minutes the rest of the guests began to arrive in Mrs. Briar's backyard: Vanessa Bender, Belinda Conrad, Brian Conrad, Biff Hooper, Tony Prito, Callie Shaw, Phil Cohen, Jerry Gilroy, and Jerry Madden, all Bayport friends the Hardys had known for years.

"I'm glad Adam Ackerman is out of town this weekend," Joe whispered to Frank. "At least we know he won't try to destroy the magic show."

"That's for sure," Frank agreed. He shook his head. "I wonder where Max is."

Just then the gate to the backyard swung open dramatically, smoke filled the air, and Max entered, dressed in his top hat and cape, a long black wand in one hand, a large cloth suitcase in the other.

"Oh, brother," Joe muttered.

"You'll have to admit that he is one cool character, though, Joe," Frank said. "You'd never believe he *dognapped* Charlie three times!"

Joe raised his hand. "Hey, Max! Over here!" he called. "We'll help you set up."

Max came over to Frank and Joe and said, "Here! Take this suitcase to my dressing room!"

Frank's nostrils flared. "Of course, Max, of course," he said, forcing a big smile. "This way."

"Would you like me to carry your wand?" Joe asked.

"Nobody touches this wand but me, Hardy," Max said.

Joe led them to the rear of the tent. "This flap is for you to come in and out unnoticed," he said. He held it open for Max. "After you," he added.

Max went inside the tent. Frank and Joe followed. A battery-powered light lit up the inside.

"When you're ready to begin the show, Max, just push this button on the CD player and your entrance music will begin," Frank said. "When you hear the French horns, that's your signal to come out onstage, so be ready. The music will shut off by itself."

"Really, Hardy, I'm not an amateur," Max said.

"We're looking forward to watching you, Max—uh, in the show, I mean," Joe said.

"Yeah," Frank agreed. "We're going to pay very close attention to *everything* you do!"

But Max was already opening up his suitcase and wasn't listening to them.

Frank found an empty seat in the back row of folding chairs, and Joe stood over by the small pond.

The music started, and then the French horns brought forth Max to the cheers of everyone in the audience.

Max did card tricks, pulled chicks and rabbits

out of his hat, made long scarves disappear, and caused his cape to turn from black to orange and back to black in the blink of an eye.

The crowd gave Max a standing ovation.

Joe looked over at Frank and gave him a *not bad* look. Frank nodded in agreement.

Suddenly Charlie started barking.

Joe looked and saw Mrs. Briar's dog coming out of the thick shrubbery that lined the back fence. He couldn't believe his eyes. *Is this Max's final trick?* he wondered.

"Charlie!" Mrs. Briar called. She hurried and picked him up. "You're back again!"

Just then the caterers arrived with the food.

"I'll show you where everything is in a minute," Mrs. Briar called.

"Where in the world did Charlie come from?" Joe said to Frank. "Do you think Max pulled a fast one on us?"

Frank thought for a minute. "No, Joe," he said. "Charlie didn't pay any attention at all to Max."

"Then that means Charlie's probably never been around Max," Joe said.

Frank nodded. He said, "Do you remember how we used to hide from each other in these shrubs?"

"Yeah! It was great!" Joe said. "But we couldn't do that very well now. They're too thick."

"For us, yeah, but not for Charlie," Frank said. "Come on. I have an idea."

Frank and Joe headed for the shrubs that bordered the part of the fence next to the alley. As best they could, they crawled in, around, and under the thick branches.

Suddenly Joe shouted, "Frank! I found it!"

Frank crawled over and looked. "A tunnel!"

"Some animal must have dug this, and then Charlie discovered it," Joe said. "He's probably been going into the alley, looking around for a while, and then coming back."

"I think we need to apologize to Max," Frank said.

"I think you do too!" a voice said.

When Frank and Joe crawled out from under the shrubs, Max was standing there.

"We apologize," Joe said. "We thought you were making Charlie disappear, since you said that you could make anything vanish."

"I accept your apology, fellows," Max said, "if you'll accept mine for wanting you to think that."

Frank and Joe grinned.

"Well, we did," Frank said. "You had us convinced that you were really that good."

"That's because I really want to be that good," Max said.

"You are, Max. You really are," Joe said.

"Didn't you hear that applause?" Frank asked. "They think you're the greatest!"

Max smiled.

"Come on!" Joe said. "We need to get something to eat before it's all gone."

"And after that we need to fill in this tunnel so Charlie won't 'disappear' again," Frank said.

"I'll help," Max said. "Maybe I can just make it 'disappear.'"

"No thanks!" Frank said. "No more magic shows for a while!"

"That's right," Joe added. "This case is closed!"